An Anthology of Poems by Anne Bronte

Anne Bronte

EasyRead Large

ReadHowYouWant Classics Library

Copyright © 2010 Accessible Publishing Systems PTY, Ltd.
ACN 085 119 953

The text in this edition has been formatted and typeset to make reading easier and more enjoyable for ALL kinds of readers. In addition the text has been formatted to the specifications indicated on the title page. The formatting of this edition is the copyright of Accessible Publishing Systems Pty Ltd.

Set in 16 pt. Verdana

ReadHowYouWant partners with publishers to provide books for ALL Kinds of Readers. For more information about Becoming A RHYW Registered Reader and to find more titles in your preferred format, visit:
www.readhowyouwant.com

Other books by Anne Bronte

Despondency and Other Poems

The Tenant of Wildfell Hall

Agnes Grey

TABLE OF CONTENTS

Poem 1: Music On Christmas Morning	1
Poem 2: A Fragment	3
Poem 3: The Student's Serenade	6
Poem 4: Home	8
Poem 5: Memory	10
Poem 6: Fluctuations	13
Poem 7: The Arbour	15
Poem 8: Dreams	17
Poem 9: If This Be All	19
Poem 10: Lines Inscribed on the Wall of A Dungeon in the Southern P of I	21
Poem 11: The Captive's Dream	23
Poem 12: A Hymn	25
Poem 13: A Prayer	28
Poem 14: Night	29
Poem 15: Call Me Away	30
Poem 16: Dreams	35
Poem 17: Confidence	37
Poem 18: Power of Love	39
Poem 19: Gloomily the Clouds	42
Poem 20: Severed and Gone	44
Poem 21: The Three Guides*	47
Poem 22: Self Communion	56
Poem 23: The Narrow Way	68
Poem 24: Verses by Lady Geralda	70
Poem 25: A Voice From the Dungeon	75

Poem 1

Music On Christmas Morning

Undated – Christmas 1841–45. Possibly 1843

Music I love – but never strain
Could kindle raptures so divine,
So grief assuage, so conquer pain,
And rouse this pensive heart of mine–
As that we hear on Christmas morn,
Upon the wintry breezes borne.

Though Darkness still her empire keep,
And hours must pass, ere morning break;
From troubled dreams, or slumbers deep,
That music KINDLY bids us wake:
It calls us, with an angel's voice,
To wake, and worship, and rejoice;

To greet with joy the glorious morn,
Which angels welcomed long ago,
When our redeeming Lord was born,
To bring the light of Heaven below;
The Powers of Darkness to dispel,
And rescue Earth from Death and Hell.

While listening to that sacred strain,
My raptured spirit soars on high;

I seem to hear those songs again
Resounding through the open sky,
That kindled such divine delight,
In those who watched their flocks by night.

With them I celebrate His birth—
Glory to God, in highest Heaven,
Good-will to men, and peace on earth,
To us a Saviour-king is given;
Our God is come to claim His own,
And Satan's power is overthrown!

A sinless God, for sinful men,
Descends to suffer and to bleed;
Hell MUST renounce its empire then;
The price is paid, the world is freed,
And Satan's self must now confess
That Christ has earned a RIGHT to bless:

Now holy Peace may smile from heaven,
And heavenly Truth from earth shall spring:
The captive's galling bonds are riven,
For our Redeemer is our king;
And He that gave his blood for men
Will lead us home to God again.

Poem 2

A Fragment

26 January 1844

Maiden, thou wert thoughtless once
Of beauty or of grace,
Simple and homely in attire
Careless of form and face.
Then whence this change, and why so oft
Dost smooth thy hazel hair?
And wherefore deck thy youthful form
With such unwearied care?
'Tell us – and cease to tire our ears
With yonder hackneyed strain–
Why wilt thou play those simple tunes
So often o'er again?'
'Nay, gentle friends, I can but say
That childhood's thoughts are gone.
Each year its own new feelings brings
And years move swiftly on,

And for these little simple airs,
I love to play them o'er–
So much I dare not promise now
To play them never more.'
I answered and it was enough;
They turned them to depart;

They could not read my secret thoughts
Nor see my throbbing heart.

I've noticed many a youthful form
Upon whose changeful face
The inmost workings of the soul
The gazer's eye might trace.
The speaking eye, the changing lip,
The ready blushing cheek,
The smiling or beclouded brow
Their different feelings speak.

But, thank God! you might gaze on mine
For hours and never know
The secret changes of my soul
From joy to bitter woe.
Last night, as we sat round the fire
Conversing merrily,
We heard without approaching steps
Of one well known to me.

There was no trembling in my voice,
No blush upon my cheek,
No lustrous sparkle in my eyes,
Of hope or joy to speak;
But O my spirit burned within,
My heart beat thick and fast.
He came not nigh – he went away
And then my joy was past.

And yet my comrades marked it not,
My voice was still the same;
They saw me smile, and o'er my face—
No signs of sadness came;
They little knew my hidden thoughts
And they will never know
The anguish of my drooping heart,
The bitter aching woe!

Poem 3

The Student's Serenade

February 1844

I have slept upon my couch,
But my spirit did not rest,
For the labours of the day
Yet my weary soul opprest;

And before my dreaming eyes
Still the learned volumes lay,
And I could not close their leaves,
And I could not turn away.

But I oped my eyes at last,
And I heard a muffled sound;
'Twas the night-breeze, come to say
That the snow was on the ground.

Then I knew that there was rest
On the mountain's bosom free;
So I left my fevered couch,
And I flew to waken thee!

I have flown to waken thee–
For, if thou wilt not arise,
Then my soul can drink no peace

From these holy moonlight skies.

And this waste of virgin snow
To my sight will not be fair,
Unless thou wilt smiling come,
Love, to wander with me there.

Then, awake! Maria, wake!
For, if thou couldst only know
How the quiet moonlight sleeps
On this wilderness of snow,

And the groves of ancient trees,
In their snowy garb arrayed,
Till they stretch into the gloom
Of the distant valley's shade;

I know thou wouldst rejoice
To inhale this bracing air;
Thou wouldst break thy sweetest sleep
To behold a scene so fair.

O'er these wintry wilds, ALONE,
Thou wouldst joy to wander free;
And it will not please thee less,
Though that bliss be shared with me.

Poem 4

Home

Undated – possibly early 1844

How brightly glistening in the sun
The woodland ivy plays!
While yonder beeches from their barks
Reflect his silver rays.

That sun surveys a lovely scene
From softly smiling skies;
And wildly through unnumbered trees
The wind of winter sighs:

Now loud, it thunders o'er my head,
And now in distance dies.
But give me back my barren hills
Where colder breezes rise;

Where scarce the scattered, stunted trees
Can yield an answering swell,
But where a wilderness of heath
Returns the sound as well.

For yonder garden, fair and wide,
With groves of evergreen,
Long winding walks, and borders trim,

And velvet lawns between;

Restore to me that little spot,
With gray walls compassed round,
Where knotted grass neglected lies,
And weeds usurp the ground.

Though all around this mansion high
Invites the foot to roam,
And though its halls are fair within—
Oh, give me back my HOME!

Poem 5

Memory

29 May 1844

Brightly the sun of summer shone
Green fields and waving woods upon,
And soft winds wandered by;
Above, a sky of purest blue,
Around, bright flowers of loveliest hue,
Allured the gazer's eye.

But what were all these charms to me,
When one sweet breath of memory
Came gently wafting by?
I closed my eyes against the day,
And called my willing soul away,
From earth, and air, and sky;

That I might simply fancy there
One little flower – a primrose fair,
Just opening into sight;
As in the days of infancy,
An opening primrose seemed to me
A source of strange delight.

Sweet Memory! ever smile on me;
Nature's chief beauties spring from thee;

Oh, still thy tribute bring
Still make the golden crocus shine
Among the flowers the most divine,
The glory of the spring.

Still in the wallflower's fragrance dwell;
And hover round the slight bluebell,
My childhood's darling flower.
Smile on the little daisy still,
The buttercup's bright goblet fill
With all thy former power.

For ever hang thy dreamy spell
Round mountain star and heather bell,
And do not pass away
From sparkling frost, or wreathed snow,
And whisper when the wild winds blow,
Or rippling waters play.

Is childhood, then, so all divine?
Or Memory, is the glory thine,
That haloes thus the past?
Not ALL divine; its pangs of grief
(Although, perchance, their stay be brief)
Are bitter while they last.

Nor is the glory all thine own,
For on our earliest joys alone
That holy light is cast.
With such a ray, no spell of thine

Can make our later pleasures shine,
Though long ago they passed.

Poem 6

Fluctuations

2 August 1844
Written at Scarborough

What though the Sun had left my sky;
To save me from despair
The blessed Moon arose on high,
And shone serenely there.

I watched her, with a tearful gaze,
Rise slowly o'er the hill,
While through the dim horizon's haze
Her light gleamed faint and chill.

I thought such wan and lifeless beams
Could ne'er my heart repay
For the bright sun's most transient gleams
That cheered me through the day:

But, as above that mist's control
She rose, and brighter shone,
I felt her light upon my soul;
But now – that light is gone!

Thick vapours snatched her from my sight,
And I was darkling left,

All in the cold and gloomy night,
Of light and hope bereft:

Until, methought, a little star
Shone forth with trembling ray,
To cheer me with its light afar–
But that, too, passed away.

Anon, an earthly meteor blazed
The gloomy darkness through;
I smiled, yet trembled while I gazed–
But that soon vanished too!

And darker, drearier fell the night
Upon my spirit then;–
But what is that faint struggling light?
Is it the Moon again?

Kind Heaven! increase that silvery gleam
And bid these clouds depart,
And let her soft celestial beam
Restore my fainting heart!

Poem 7

The Arbour

Undated −1840 to early 1845

I'll rest me in this sheltered bower,
And look upon the clear blue sky
That smiles upon me through the trees,
Which stand so thick clustering by;

And view their green and glossy leaves,
All glistening in the sunshine fair;
And list the rustling of their boughs,
So softly whispering through the air.

And while my ear drinks in the sound,
My winged soul shall fly away;
Reviewing lone departed years
As one mild, beaming, autumn day;

And soaring on to future scenes,
Like hills and woods, and valleys green,
All basking in the summer's sun,
But distant still, and dimly seen.

Oh, list! 'tis summer's very breath
That gently shakes the rustling trees−
But look! the snow is on the ground−

How can I think of scenes like these?

'Tis but the FROST that clears the air,
And gives the sky that lovely blue;
They're smiling in a WINTER'S sun,
Those evergreens of sombre hue.

And winter's chill is on my heart–
How can I dream of future bliss?
How can my spirit soar away,
Confined by such a chain as this?

Poem 8

Dreams

Spring 1845

While on my lonely couch I lie,
I seldom feel myself alone,
For fancy fills my dreaming eye
With scenes and pleasures of its own.

Then I may cherish at my breast
An infant's form beloved and fair,
May smile and soothe it into rest
With all a Mother's fondest care.

How sweet to feel its helpless form
Depending thus on me alone!
And while I hold it safe and warm
What bliss to think it is my own!

And glances then may meet my eyes
That daylight never showed to me;
What raptures in my bosom rise,
Those earnest looks of love to see,

To feel my hand so kindly prest,
To know myself beloved at last,
To think my heart has found a rest,

My life of solitude is past!

But then to wake and find it flown,
The dream of happiness destroyed,
To find myself unloved, alone,
What tongue can speak the dreary void?

A heart whence warm affections flow,
Creator, thou hast given to me,
And am I only thus to know
How sweet the joys of love would be?

Poem 9

If This Be All

20 May 1845

O God! if this indeed be all
That Life can show to me;
If on my aching brow may fall
No freshening dew from Thee;

If with no brighter light than this
The lamp of hope may glow,
And I may only dream of bliss,
And wake to weary woe;

If friendship's solace must decay,
When other joys are gone,
And love must keep so far away,
While I go wandering on,–

Wandering and toiling without gain,
The slave of others' will,
With constant care, and frequent pain,
Despised, forgotten still;

Grieving to look on vice and sin,
Yet powerless to quell
The silent current from within,

The outward torrent's swell

While all the good I would impart,
The feelings I would share,
Are driven backward to my heart,
And turned to wormwood there;

If clouds must EVER keep from sight
The glories of the Sun,
And I must suffer Winter's blight,
Ere Summer is begun

If Life must be so full of care,
Then call me soon to thee;
Or give me strength enough to bear
My load of misery.

Poem 10

Lines Inscribed on the Wall of A Dungeon in the Southern P of I

16 December 1844

Though not a breath can enter here,
I know the wind blows fresh and free;
I know the sun is shining clear,
Though not a gleam can visit me.

They thought while I in darkness lay,
'Twere pity that I should not know
How all the earth is smiling gay;
How fresh the vernal breezes blow.

They knew, such tidings to impart
Would pierce my weary spirit through,
And could they better read my heart,
They'd tell me, she was smiling too.

They need not, for I know it well,
Methinks I see her even now;
No sigh disturbs her bosom's swell,
No shade o'ercasts her angel brow.

Unmarred by grief her angel voice,
Whence sparkling wit, and wisdom flow:
And others in its sound rejoice,
And taste the joys I must not know,

Drink rapture from her soft dark eye,
And sunshine from her heavenly smile;
On wings of bliss their moments fly,
And I am pining here the while!

Oh! tell me, does she never give–
To my distress a single sigh?
She smiles on them, but does she grieve
One moment, when they are not by?

When she beholds the sunny skies,
And feels the wind of heaven blow;
Has she no tear for him that lies
In dungeon gloom, so far below?

While others gladly round her press
And at her side their hours beguile,
Has she no sigh for his distress
Who cannot see a single smile

Nor hear one word nor read a line
That her beloved hand might write,
Who banished from her face must pine
Each day a long and lonely night?

Poem 11

The Captive's Dream

Methought I saw him but I knew him not;
He was so changed from what he used to be,
There was no redness on his woe-worn cheek,
No sunny smile upon his ashy lips,
His hollow wandering eyes looked wild and fierce,
And grief was printed on his marble brow,
And O I thought he clasped his wasted hands,
And raised his haggard eyes to Heaven, and
 prayed
That he might die – I had no power to speak,
I thought I was allowed to see him thus;
And yet I might not speak one single word;
I might not even tell him that I lived
And that it might be possible if search were made,
To find out where I was and set me free,
O how I longed to clasp him to my heart,
Or but to hold his trembling hand in mine,
And speak one word of comfort to his mind,
I struggled wildly but it was in vain,
I could not rise from my dark dungeon floor,
And the dear name I vainly strove to speak,
Died in a voiceless whisper on my tongue,
Then I awoke, and lo it was a dream!
A dream? Alas it was reality!
For well I know wherever he may be

He mourns me thus – O heaven I could bear
My deadly fate with calmness if there were
No kindred hearts to bleed and break for me!

Poem 12

A Hymn

Eternal power of earth and air,
Unseen, yet seen in all around,
Remote, but dwelling everywhere,
Though silent, heard in every sound.

If e'er thine ear in mercy bent
When wretched mortals cried to thee,
And if indeed thy Son was sent
To save lost sinners such as me.

Then hear me now, while kneeling here;
I lift to thee my heart and eye
And all my soul ascends in prayer;
O give me – give me Faith I cry.

Without some glimmering in my heart,
I could not raise this fervent prayer;
But O a stronger light impart,
And in thy mercy fix it there!

While Faith is with me I am blest;
It turns my darkest night to day;
But while I clasp it to my breast
I often feel it slide away.

Then cold and dark my spirit sinks,
To see my light of life depart,
And every fiend of Hell methinks
Enjoys the anguish of my heart.

What shall I do if all my love,
My hopes, my toil, are cast away,
And if there be no God above
To hear and bless me when I pray?

If this be vain delusion all,
If death be an eternal sleep,
And none can hear my secret call,
Or see the silent tears I weep.

O help me God! for thou alone
Canst my distracted soul relieve;
Forsake it not – it is thine own,
Though weak yet longing to believe.

O drive these cruel doubts away
And make me know that thou art God;
A Faith that shines by night and day
Will lighten every earthly load.

If I believe that Jesus died
And waking rose to reign above,
Then surely Sorrow, Sin and Pride
Must yield to peace and hope and love.

And all the blessed words he said
Will strength and holy joy impart,
A shield of safety o'er my head,
A spring of comfort in my heart.

Poem 13

A Prayer

My God (oh, let me call Thee mine,
Weak, wretched sinner though I be),
My trembling soul would fain be Thine;
My feeble faith still clings to Thee.

Not only for the Past I grieve,
The Future fills me with dismay;
Unless Thou hasten to relieve,
Thy suppliant is a castaway.

I cannot say my faith is strong,
I dare not hope my love is great;
But strength and love to Thee belong;
Oh, do not leave me desolate!

I know I owe my all to Thee;
Oh, TAKE the heart I cannot give!
Do Thou my strength – my Saviour be,
And MAKE me to Thy glory live.

Poem 14

Night

I love the silent hour of night,
For blissful dreams may then arise,
Revealing to my charmed sight
What may not bless my waking eyes!

And then a voice may meet my ear
That death has silenced long ago;
And hope and rapture may appear
Instead of solitude and woe.

Cold in the grave for years has lain
The form it was my bliss to see,
And only dreams can bring again
The darling of my heart to me.

Poem 15

Call Me Away

Call me away; there's nothing here,
That wins my soul to stay;
Then let me leave this prospect drear,
And hasten far away.

To our beloved land I'll flee,
Our land of thought and soul,
Where I have roved so oft with thee,
Beyond the world's control.

I'll sit and watch those ancient trees,
Those Scotch firs dark and high;
I'll listen to the eerie breeze,
Among their branches sigh.

The glorious moon shines far above;
How soft her radiance falls,
On snowy heights, and rock, and grove;
And yonder palace walls!

Who stands beneath yon fir trees high?
A youth both slight and fair,
Whose bright and restless azure eye
Proclaims him known to care,
Though fair that brow, it is not smooth;

Though small those features, yet in sooth
Stern passion has been there.

Now on the peaceful moon are fixed
Those eyes so glistening bright,
But trembling teardrops hang betwixt,
And dim the blessed light.

Though late the hour, and keen the blast,
That whistles round him now,
Those raven locks are backward cast,
To cool his burning brow.

His hands above his heaving breast
Are clasped in agony
'O Father! Father! let me rest!
And call my soul to thee!

'I know 'tis weakness thus to pray;
But all this cankering care–
This doubt tormenting night and day
Is more than I can bear!

'I'll sit and watch those ancient trees,
Those Scotch firs dark and high;
I'll listen to the eerie breeze,
Among their branches sigh.'

The glorious moon shines far above;
How soft her radiance falls,

On snowy heights, and rock, and grove;
And yonder palace walls!

Who stands beneath yon fir trees high?
A youth both slight and fair,
Whose bright and restless azure eye
Proclaims him known to care,
Though fair that brow, it is not smooth;
Though small those features, yet in sooth
Stern passion has been there.

Now on the peaceful moon are fixed
Those eyes so glistening bright,
But trembling teardrops hang betwixt,
And dim the blessed light.

Though late the hour, and keen the blast,
That whistles round him now,
Those raven locks are backward cast,
To cool his burning brow.

His hands above his heaving breast
Are clasped in agony–
'O Father! Father! let me rest!
And call my soul to thee!

'I know 'tis weakness thus to pray;
But all this cankering care–
This doubt tormenting night and day
Is more than I can bear!

'With none to comfort, none to guide
And none to strengthen me.
Since thou my only friend hast died—
I've pined to follow thee!
Since thou hast died! And did he live
What comfort could his counsel give—
To one forlorn like me?

'Would he my Idol's form adore—
Her soul, her glance, her tone?
And say, "Forget for ever more
Her kindred and thine own;
Let dreams of her thy peace destroy,
Leave every other hope and joy
And live for her alone"?'

'He starts, he smiles, and dries the tears,
Still glistening on his cheek,
The lady of his soul appears,
And hark! I hear her speak—

'Aye, dry thy tears; thou wilt not weep—
While I am by thy side—
Our foes all day their watch may keep
But cannot thus divide
Such hearts as ours; and we tonight
Together in the clear moon's light
Their malice will deride.

'No fear our present bliss shall blast

And sorrow we'll defy.
Do thou forget the dreary past,
The dreadful future I.'

Forget it? Yes, while thou art by
I think of nought but thee,
'Tis only when thou art not nigh
Remembrance tortures me.

But such a lofty soul to find,
And such a heart as thine,
In such a glorious form enshrined
And still to call thee mine–
Would be for earth too great a bliss,
Without a taint of woe like this,
Then why should I repine?

Poem 16

Dreams

While on my lonely couch I lie,
I seldom feel myself alone,
For fancy fills my dreaming eye
With scenes and pleasures of its own.

Then I may cherish at my breast
An infant's form beloved and fair,
May smile and soothe it into rest
With all a Mother's fondest care.

How sweet to feel its helpless form
Depending thus on me alone!
And while I hold it safe and warm
What bliss to think it is my own!

And glances then may meet my eyes
That daylight never showed to me;
What raptures in my bosom rise,
Those earnest looks of love to see,

To feel my hand so kindly prest,
To know myself beloved at last,
To think my heart has found a rest,
My life of solitude is past!

But then to wake and find it flown,
The dream of happiness destroyed,
To find myself unloved, alone,
What tongue can speak the dreary void?

A heart whence warm affections flow,
Creator, thou hast given to me,
And am I only thus to know
How sweet the joys of love would be?

Poem 17

Confidence

Oppressed with sin and woe,
A burdened heart I bear,
Opposed by many a mighty foe;
But I will not despair.

With this polluted heart,
I dare to come to Thee,
Holy and mighty as Thou art,
For Thou wilt pardon me.

I feel that I am weak,
And prone to every sin;
But Thou who giv'st to those who seek,
Wilt give me strength within.

Far as this earth may be
From yonder starry skies;
Remoter still am I from Thee:
Yet Thou wilt not despise.

I need not fear my foes,
I deed not yield to care;
I need not sink beneath my woes,
For Thou wilt answer prayer.

In my Redeemer's name,
I give myself to Thee;
And, all unworthy as I am,
My God will cherish me.

Poem 18

Power of Love

Love, indeed thy strength is mighty
Thus, alone, such strife to bear
Three 'gainst one, and never ceasing
Death, and Madness, and Despair!

'Tis not my own strength has saved me;
Health, and hope, and fortitude,
But for love, had long since failed me;
Heart and soul had sunk subdued.

Often, in my wild impatience,
I have lost my trust in Heaven,
And my soul has tossed and struggled,
Like a vessel tempest-driven;

But the voice of my beloved
In my ear has seemed to say
'O, be patient if thou lov'st me!'
And the storm has passed away.

When outworn with weary thinking,
Sight and thought were waxing dim,
And my mind began to wander,
And my brain began to swim,

Then those hands outstretched to save me
Seemed to call me back again
Those dark eyes did so implore me
To resume my reason's reign,

That I could not but remember
How her hopes were fixed on me,
And, with one determined effort,
Rose, and shook my spirit free.

When hope leaves my weary spirit
All the power to hold it gone
That loved voice so loudly prays me,
'For my sake, keep hoping on,'

That, at once my strength renewing,
Though Despair had crushed me down,
I can burst his bonds asunder,
And defy his deadliest frown.

When, from nights of restless tossing,
Days of gloom and pining care,
Pain and weakness, still increasing,
Seem to whisper 'Death is near,'

And I almost bid him welcome,
Knowing he would bring release,
Weary of this restless struggle
Longing to repose in peace,

Then a glance of fond reproval
Bids such selfish longings flee
And a voice of matchless music
Murmurs 'Cherish life for me!'

Roused to newborn strength and courage,
Pain and grief, I cast away,
Health and life, I keenly follow,
Mighty Death is held at bay.

Yes, my love, I will be patient!
Firm and bold my heart shall be:
Fear not – though this life is dreary,
I can bear it well for thee.

Let our foes still rain upon me
Cruel wrongs and taunting scorn;
'Tis for thee their hate pursues me,
And for thee, it shall be borne!

Poem 19

Gloomily the Clouds

Gloomily the clouds are sailing
O'er the dimly moonlit sky;
Dolefully the wind is wailing;
Not another sound is nigh;

Only I can hear it sweeping
Heathclad hill and woodland dale,
And at times the nights's sad weeping
Sounds above its dying wail.

Now the struggling moonbeams glimmer;
Now the shadows deeper fall,
Till the dim light, waxing dimmer,
Scarce reveals yon stately hall.

All beneath its roof are sleeping;
Such a silence reigns around
I can hear the cold rain steeping
Dripping roof and plashy ground.

No: not all are wrapped in slumber;
At yon chamber window stands
One whose years can scarce outnumber
The tears that dew his clasped hands.

From the open casement bending
He surveys the murky skies,
Dreary sighs his bosom rending;
Hot tears gushing from his eyes.

Now that Autumn's charms are dying,
Summer's glories long since gone,
Faded leaves on damp earth lying,
Hoary winter striding on,–

'Tis no marvel skies are lowering,
Winds are moaning thus around,
And cold rain, with ceaseless pouring,
Swells the streams and swamps the ground;

But such wild, such bitter grieving
Fits not slender boys like thee;
Such deep sighs should not be heaving
Breasts so young as thine must be.

Life with thee is only springing;
Summer in thy pathway lies;
Every day is nearer bringing
June's bright flowers and glowing skies.

Ah, he sees no brighter morrow!
He is not too young to prove
All the pain and all the sorrow
That attend the steps of love.

Poem 20

Severed and Gone

Severed and gone, so many years!
And art thou still so dear to me,
That throbbing heart and burning tears
Can witness how I cling to thee?

I know that in the narrow tomb
The form I loved was buried deep,
And left, in silence and in gloom,
To slumber out its dreamless sleep.

I know the corner where it lies,
Is but a dreary place of rest:
The charnel moisture never dries
From the dark flagstones o'er its breast,

For there the sunbeams never shine,
Nor ever breathes the freshening air,
– But not for this do I repine;
For my beloved is not there.

O, no! I do not think of thee
As festering there in slow decay:
'Tis this sole thought oppresses me,
That thou art gone so far away.

For ever gone; for I, by night,
Have prayed, within my silent room,
That Heaven would grant a burst of light
Its cheerless darkness to illume;

And give thee to my longing eyes,
A moment, as thou shinest now,
Fresh from thy mansion in the skies,
With all its glories on thy brow.

Wild was the wish, intense the gaze
I fixed upon the murky air,
Expecting, half, a kindling blaze
Would strike my raptured vision there,

A shape these human nerves would thrill,
A majesty that might appal,
Did not thy earthly likeness, still,
Gleam softly, gladly, through it all.

False hope! vain prayer! it might not be
That thou shouldst visit earth again.
I called on Heaven – I called on thee,
And watched, and waited – all in vain.

Had I one shining tress of thine,
How it would bless these longing eyes!
Or if thy pictured form were mine,
What gold should rob me of the prize?

A few cold words on yonder stone,
A corpse as cold as they can be—
Vain words, and mouldering dust, alone—
Can this be all that's left of thee?

O, no! thy spirit lingers still
Where'er thy sunny smile was seen:
There's less of darkness, less of chill
On earth, than if thou hadst not been.

Thou breathest in my bosom yet,
And dwellest in my beating heart;
And, while I cannot quite forget,
Thou, darling, canst not quite depart.

Though, freed from sin, and grief, and pain
Thou drinkest now the bliss of Heaven,
Thou didst not visit earth in vain;
And from us, yet, thou art not riven.

Life seems more sweet that thou didst live,
And men more true that thou wert one:
Nothing is lost that thou didst give,
Nothing destroyed that thou hast done.

Earth hath received thine earthly part;
Thine heavenly flame has heavenward flown;
But both still linger in my heart,
Still live, and not in mine alone.

Poem 21

The Three Guides*

[* First published in FRASER'S MAGAZINE.]

Spirit of Earth! thy hand is chill:
I've felt its icy clasp;
And, shuddering, I remember still
That stony-hearted grasp.
Thine eye bids love and joy depart:
Oh, turn its gaze from me!
It presses down my shrinking heart;
I will not walk with thee!

"Wisdom is mine," I've heard thee say:
"Beneath my searching eye
All mist and darkness melt away,
Phantoms and fables fly.
Before me truth can stand alone,
The naked, solid truth;
And man matured by worth will own,
If I am shunned by youth.

"Firm is my tread, and sure though slow;
My footsteps never slide;
And he that follows me shall know
I am the surest guide."
Thy boast is vain; but were it true

That thou couldst safely steer
Life's rough and devious pathway through,
Such guidance I should fear.

How could I bear to walk for aye,
With eyes to earthward prone,
O'er trampled weeds and miry clay,
And sand and flinty stone;
Never the glorious view to greet
Of hill and dale, and sky;
To see that Nature's charms are sweet,
Or feel that Heaven is nigh?

If in my heart arose a spring,
A gush of thought divine,
At once stagnation thou wouldst bring
With that cold touch of thine.
If, glancing up, I sought to snatch
But one glimpse of the sky,
My baffled gaze would only catch
Thy heartless, cold grey eye.

If to the breezes wandering near,
I listened eagerly,
And deemed an angel's tongue to hear
That whispered hope to me,
That heavenly music would be drowned
In thy harsh, droning voice;
Nor inward thought, nor sight, nor sound,
Might my sad soul rejoice.

Dull is thine ear, unheard by thee
The still, small voice of Heaven;
Thine eyes are dim and cannot see
The helps that God has given.
There is a bridge o'er every flood
Which thou canst not perceive;
A path through every tangled wood,
But thou wilt not believe.

Striving to make thy way by force,
Toil-spent and bramble-torn,
Thou'lt fell the tree that checks thy course,
And burst through brier and thorn:
And, pausing by the river's side,
Poor reasoner! thou wilt deem,
By casting pebbles in its tide,
To cross the swelling stream.

Right through the flinty rock thou'lt try
Thy toilsome way to bore,
Regardless of the pathway nigh
That would conduct thee o'er
Not only art thou, then, unkind,
And freezing cold to me,
But unbelieving, deaf, and blind:
I will not walk with thee!

Spirit of Pride! thy wings are strong,
Thine eyes like lightning shine;
Ecstatic joys to thee belong,

And powers almost divine.
But 'tis a false, destructive blaze
Within those eyes I see;
Turn hence their fascinating gaze;
I will not follow thee.

"Coward and fool!" thou mayst reply,
Walk on the common sod;
Go, trace with timid foot and eye
The steps by others trod.
'Tis best the beaten path to keep,
The ancient faith to hold;
To pasture with thy fellow-sheep,
And lie within the fold.

Cling to the earth, poor grovelling worm;
'Tis not for thee to soar
Against the fury of the storm,
Amid the thunder's roar!
There's glory in that daring strife
Unknown, undreamt by thee;
There's speechless rapture in the life
Of those who follow me.

Yes, I have seen thy votaries oft,
Upheld by thee their guide,
In strength and courage mount aloft
The steepy mountain-side;
I've seen them stand against the sky,
And gazing from below,

Beheld thy lightning in their eye
Thy triumph on their brow.

Oh, I have felt what glory then,
What transport must be theirs!
So far above their fellow-men,
Above their toils and cares;
Inhaling Nature's purest breath,
Her riches round them spread,
The wide expanse of earth beneath,
Heaven's glories overhead!

But I have seen them helpless, dash'd
Down to a bloody grave,
And still thy ruthless eye has flash'd,
Thy strong hand did not save;
I've seen some o'er the mountain's brow
Sustain'd awhile by thee,
O'er rocks of ice and hills of snow
Bound fearless, wild, and free.

Bold and exultant was their mien,
While thou didst cheer them on;
But evening fell, – and then, I ween,
Their faithless guide was gone.
Alas! how fared thy favourites then,–
Lone, helpless, weary, cold?
Did ever wanderer find again
The path he left of old?

Where is their glory, where the pride
That swelled their hearts before?
Where now the courage that defied
The mightiest tempest's roar?
What shall they do when night grows black,
When angry storms arise?
Who now will lead them to the track
Thou taught'st them to despise?

Spirit of Pride, it needs not this
To make me shun thy wiles,
Renounce thy triumph and thy bliss,
Thy honours and thy smiles!
Bright as thou art, and bold, and strong,
That fierce glance wins not me,
And I abhor thy scoffing tongue–
I will not follow thee!

Spirit of Faith! be thou my guide,
O clasp my hand in thine,
And let me never quit thy side;
Thy comforts are divine!
Earth calls thee blind, misguided one,–
But who can shew like thee
Forgotten things that have been done,
And things that are to be?

Secrets conceal'd from Nature's ken,
Who like thee can declare?
Or who like thee to erring men

God's holy will can bear?
Pride scorns thee for thy lowly mien,—
But who like thee can rise
Above this toilsome, sordid scene,
Beyond the holy skies?

Meek is thine eye and soft thy voice,
But wondrous is thy might,
To make the wretched soul rejoice,
To give the simple light!
And still to all that seek thy way
This magic power is given,—
E'en while their footsteps press the clay,
Their souls ascend to heaven.

Danger surrounds them, — pain and woe
Their portion here must be,
But only they that trust thee know
What comfort dwells with thee;
Strength to sustain their drooping pow'rs,
And vigour to defend,—
Thou pole-star of my darkest hours
Affliction's firmest friend!

Day does not always mark our way,
Night's shadows oft appal,
But lead me, and I cannot stray,—
Hold me, I shall not fall;
Sustain me, I shall never faint,
How rough soe'er may be

My upward road, – nor moan, nor plaint
Shall mar my trust in thee.

Narrow the path by which we go,
And oft it turns aside
From pleasant meads where roses blow,
And peaceful waters glide;
Where flowery turf lies green and soft,
And gentle gales are sweet,
To where dark mountains frown aloft,
Hard rocks distress the feet,–

Deserts beyond lie bleak and bare,
And keen winds round us blow;
But if thy hand conducts me there,
The way is right, I know.
I have no wish to turn away;
My spirit does not quail,–
How can it while I hear thee say,
"Press forward and prevail!"

Even above the tempest's swell
I hear thy voice of love,–
Of hope and peace, I hear thee tell,
And that blest home above;
Through pain and death I can rejoice.
If but thy strength be mine,–
Earth hath no music like thy voice,
Life owns no joy like thine!

Spirit of Faith, I'll go with thee!
Thou, if I hold thee fast,
Wilt guide, defend, and strengthen me,
And bear me home at last;
By thy help all things I can do,
In thy strength all things bear,–
Teach me, for thou art just and true,
Smile on me, thou art fair!

Poem 22

Self Communion

'The mist is resting on the hill;
The smoke is hanging in the air;
The very clouds are standing still:
A breathless calm broods everywhere.
Thou pilgrim through this vale of tears,
Thou, too, a little moment cease
Thy anxious toil and fluttering fears,
And rest thee, for a while, in peace.'

'I would, but Time keeps working still
And moving on for good or ill:
He will not rest or stay.
In pain or ease, in smiles or tears,
He still keeps adding to my years
And stealing life away.
His footsteps in the ceaseless sound
Of yonder clock I seem to hear,
That through this stillness so profound
Distinctly strikes the vacant ear.
For ever striding on and on,
He pauses not by night or day;
And all my life will soon be gone
As these past years have slipped away.
He took my childhood long ago,
And then my early youth; and lo,

He steals away my prime!
I cannot see how fast it goes,
But well my inward spirit knows
The wasting power of time.'

'Time steals thy moments, drinks thy breath,
Changes and wastes thy mortal frame;
But though he gives the clay to death,
He cannot touch the inward flame.
Nay, though he steals thy years away,
Their memory is left thee still,
And every month and every day
Leaves some effect of good or ill.
The wise will find in Memory's store
A help for that which lies before
To guide their course aright;
Then, hush thy plaints and calm thy fears;
Look back on these departed years,
And, say, what meets thy sight?'

'I see, far back, a helpless child,
Feeble and full of causeless fears,
Simple and easily beguiled
To credit all it hears.
More timid than the wild wood-dove,
Yet trusting to another's care,
And finding in protecting love
Its only refuge from despair,–
Its only balm for every woe,
The only bliss its soul can know;–

Still hiding in its breast.
A tender heart too prone to weep,
A love so earnest, strong, and deep
It could not be expressed.

'Poor helpless thing! what can it do
Life's stormy cares and toils among;–
How tread this weary desert through
That awes the brave and tires the strong?
Where shall it centre so much trust
Where truth maintains so little sway,
Where seeming fruit is bitter dust,
And kisses oft to death betray?
How oft must sin and falsehood grieve
A heart so ready to believe,
And willing to admire!
With strength so feeble, fears so strong,
Amid this selfish bustling throng,
How will it faint and tire!

'That tender love so warm and deep,
How can it flourish here below?
What bitter floods of tears must steep
The stony soil where it would grow!
O earth! a rocky breast is thine–

'A hard soil and a cruel clime,
Where tender plants must droop and pine,
Or alter with transforming time.
That soul, that clings to sympathy,

As ivy clasps the forest tree,
How can it stand alone?
That heart so prone to overflow
E'en at the thought of others' woe,
How will it bear its own?

'How, if a sparrow's death can wring
Such bitter tear-floods from the eye,
Will it behold the suffering
Of struggling, lost humanity?
The torturing pain, the pining grief,
The sin-degraded misery,
The anguish that defies relief?'

'Look back again – What dost thou see?'

'I see one kneeling on the sod,
With infant hands upraised to Heaven,
A young heart feeling after God,
Oft baffled, never backward driven.
Mistaken oft, and oft astray,
It strives to find the narrow way,
But gropes and toils alone:
That inner life of strife and tears,
Of kindling hopes and lowering fears
To none but God is known.
'Tis better thus; for man would scorn
Those childish prayers, those artless cries,
That darkling spirit tossed and torn,
But God will not despise!

We may regret such waste of tears
Such darkly toiling misery,
Such 'wildering doubts and harrowing fears,
Where joy and thankfulness should be;
But wait, and Heaven will send relief.
Let patience have her perfect work:
Lo, strength and wisdom spring from grief,
And joys behind afflictions lurk!

'It asked for light, and it is heard;
God grants that struggling soul repose
And, guided by His holy word,
It wiser than its teachers grows.
It gains the upward path at length,
And passes on from strength to strength,
Leaning on Heaven the while:
Night's shades departing one by one,
It sees at last the rising sun,
And feels his cheering smile.
In all its darkness and distress
For light it sought, to God it cried;
And through the pathless wilderness,
He was its comfort and its guide.'

'So was it, and so will it be:
Thy God will guide and strengthen thee;
His goodness cannot fail.
The sun that on thy morning rose
Will light thee to the evening's close,
Whatever storms assail.'

'God alters not; but Time on me
A wide and wondrous change has wrought:
And in these parted years I see
Cause for grave care and saddening thought.
I see that time, and toil, and truth,
An inward hardness can impart,–
Can freeze the generous blood of youth,
And steel full fast the tender heart.'

'Bless God for that divine decree!–
That hardness comes with misery,
And suffering deadens pain;
That at the frequent sight of woe
E'en Pity's tears forget to flow,
If reason still remain!
Reason, with conscience by her side,
But gathers strength from toil and truth;
And she will prove a surer guide
Than those sweet instincts of our youth.
Thou that hast known such anguish sore
In weeping where thou couldst not bless,
Canst thou that softness so deplore–
That suffering, shrinking tenderness?
Thou that hast felt what cankering care
A loving heart is doomed to bear,
Say, how canst thou regret
That fires unfed must fall away,
Long droughts can dry the softest clay,
And cold will cold beget?'

'Nay, but 'tis hard to feel that chill
Come creeping o'er the shuddering heart.
Love may be full of pain, but still,
'Tis sad to see it so depart,–
To watch that fire whose genial glow
Was formed to comfort and to cheer,
For want of fuel, fading so,
Sinking to embers dull and drear,–
To see the soft soil turned to stone
For lack of kindly showers,–
To see those yearnings of the breast,
Pining to bless and to be blessed,
Drop withered, frozen one by one,
Till, centred in itself alone,
It wastes its blighted powers.

'Oh, I have known a wondrous joy
In early friendship's pure delight,–
A genial bliss that could not cloy–
My sun by day, my moon by night.
Absence, indeed, was sore distress,
And thought of death was anguish keen,
And there was cruel bitterness
When jarring discords rose between;
And sometimes it was grief to know
My fondness was but half returned.
But this was nothing to the woe
With which another truth was learned:–
That I must check, or nurse apart,
Full many an impulse of the heart

And many a darling thought:
What my soul worshipped, sought, and prized,
Were slighted, questioned, or despised;–
This pained me more than aught.
And as my love the warmer glowed
The deeper would that anguish sink,
That this dark stream between us flowed,
Though both stood bending o'er its brink;
Until, as last, I learned to bear
A colder heart within my breast;
To share such thoughts as I could share,
And calmly keep the rest.
I saw that they were sundered now,
The trees that at the root were one:
They yet might mingle leaf and bough,
But still the stems must stand alone.

'O love is sweet of every kind!
'Tis sweet the helpless to befriend,
To watch the young unfolding mind,
To guide, to shelter, and defend:
To lavish tender toil and care,
And ask for nothing back again,
But that our smiles a blessing bear
And all our toil be not in vain.
And sweeter far than words can tell
Their love whose ardent bosoms swell
With thoughts they need not hide;
Where fortune frowns not on their joy,
And Prudence seeks not to destroy,

Nor Reason to deride.

'Whose love may freely gush and flow,
Unchecked, unchilled by doubt or fear,
For in their inmost hearts they know
It is not vainly nourished there.
They know that in a kindred breast
Their long desires have found a home,
Where heart and soul may kindly rest,
Weary and lorn no more to roam.
Their dreams of bliss were not in vain,
As they love they are loved again,
And they can bless as they are blessed.

'O vainly might I seek to show
The joys from happy love that flow!
The warmest words are all too cold
The secret transports to unfold
Of simplest word or softest sigh,
Or from the glancing of an eye
To say what rapture beams;
One look that bids our fears depart,
And well assures the trusting heart.
It beats not in the world alone–
Such speechless rapture I have known,
But only in my dreams.

'My life has been a morning sky
Where Hope her rainbow glories cast
O'er kindling vapours far and nigh:

And, if the colours faded fast,
Ere one bright hue had died away
Another o'er its ashes gleamed;
And if the lower clouds were grey,
The mists above more brightly beamed.
But not for long; – at length behold,
Those tints less warm, less radiant grew;
Till but one streak of paly gold
Glimmered through clouds of saddening hue.
And I am calmly waiting, now,
To see that also pass away,
And leave, above the dark hill's brow,
A rayless arch of sombre grey.'

'So must it fare with all thy race
Who seek in earthly things their joy:
So fading hopes lost hopes shall chase
Till Disappointment all destroy.
But they that fix their hopes on high
Shall, in the blue-refulgent sky,
The sun's transcendent light,
Behold a purer, deeper glow
Than these uncertain gleams can show,
However fair or bright.
O weak of heart! why thus deplore
That Truth will Fancy's dreams destroy?
Did I not tell thee, years before,
Life was for labour, not for joy?
Cease, selfish spirit, to repine;
O'er thine own ills no longer grieve;

Lo, there are sufferings worse than thine,
Which thou mayst labour to relieve.
If Time indeed too swiftly flies,
Gird on thine armour, haste, arise,
For thou hast much to do;–
To lighten woe, to trample sin,
And foes without and foes within
To combat and subdue.
Earth hath too much of sin and pain:
The bitter cup – the binding chain
Dost thou indeed lament?
Let not thy weary spirit sink;
But strive – not by one drop or link
The evil to augment.
Strive rather thou, by peace and joy,
The bitter poison to destroy,
The cruel chain to break.
O strive! and if thy strength be small,
Strive yet the more, and spend it all
For Love and Wisdom's sake!'

'O I have striven both hard and long
But many are my foes and strong.
My gains are light – my progress slow;
For hard's the way I have to go,
And my worst enemies, I know,
Are these within my breast;
And it is hard to toil for aye,–
Through sultry noon and twilight grey
To toil and never rest.'

'There is a rest beyond the grave,
A lasting rest from pain and sin,
Where dwell the faithful and the brave;
But they must strive who seek to win.'
Show me that rest – I ask no more.
Oh, drive these misty doubts away;
And let me see that sunny shore,
However far away!
However wide this rolling sea,
However wild my passage be,
Howe'er my bark be tempest tossed,
May it but reach that haven fair,
May I but land and wander there,
With those that I have loved and lost:
With such a glorious hope in view,
I'll gladly toil and suffer too.
Rest without toil I would not ask;
I would not shun the hardest task:
Toil is my glory – Grief my gain,
If God's approval they obtain.
Could I but hear my Saviour say,–
"I know thy patience and thy love;
How thou hast held the narrow way,
For my sake laboured night and day,
And watched, and striven with them that strove;
And still hast borne, and didst not faint,"–
Oh, this would be reward indeed!'

'Press forward, then, without complaint;
Labour and love – and such shall be thy meed.'

Poem 23

The Narrow Way

Believe not those who say
The upward path is smooth,
Lest thou shouldst stumble in the way,
And faint before the truth.

It is the only road
Unto the realms of joy;
But he who seeks that blest abode
Must all his powers employ.

Bright hopes and pure delight
Upon his course may beam,
And there, amid the sternest heights,
The sweetest flowerets gleam.

On all her breezes borne,
Earth yields no scents like those;
But he that dares not gasp the thorn
Should never crave the rose.

Arm – arm thee for the fight!
Cast useless loads away;
Watch through the darkest hours of night;
Toil through the hottest day.

Crush pride into the dust,
Or thou must needs be slack;
And trample down rebellious lust,
Or it will hold thee back.

Seek not thy honour here;
Waive pleasure and renown;
The world's dread scoff undaunted bear,
And face its deadliest frown.

To labour and to love,
To pardon and endure,
To lift thy heart to God above,
And keep thy conscience pure;

Be this thy constant aim,
Thy hope, thy chief delight;
What matter who should whisper blame
Or who should scorn or slight?

What matter, if thy God approve,
And if, within thy breast,
Thou feel the comfort of His love,
The earnest of His rest?

Poem 24

Verses by Lady Geralda

Why, when I hear the stormy breath
Of the wild winter wind
Rushing o'er the mountain heath,
Does sadness fill my mind?

For long ago I loved to lie
Upon the pathless moor,
To hear the wild wind rushing by
With never ceasing roar;

Its sound was music then to me;
Its wild and lofty voice
Made by heart beat exultingly
And my whole soul rejoice.

But now, how different is the sound?
It takes another tone,
And howls along the barren ground
With melancholy moan.

Why does the warm light of the sun
No longer cheer my eyes?
And why is all the beauty gone
From rosy morning skies?

Beneath this lone and dreary hill
There is a lovely vale;
The purling of a crystal rill,
The sighing of the gale,

The sweet voice of the singing bird,
The wind among the trees,
Are ever in that valley heard;
While every passing breeze

Is loaded with the pleasant scent
Of wild and lovely flowers.
To yonder vales I often went
To pass my evening hours.

Last evening when I wandered there
To soothe my weary heart,
Why did the unexpected tear
From my sad eyelid start?

Why did the trees, the buds, the stream
Sing forth so joylessly?
And why did all the valley seem
So sadly changed to me?

I plucked a primrose young and pale
That grew beneath a tree
And then I hastened from the vale
Silent and thoughtfully.

Soon I was near my lofty home,
But when I cast my eye
Upon that flower so fair and lone
Why did I heave a sigh?

I thought of taking it again
To the valley where it grew.
But soon I spurned that thought as vain
And weak and childish too.

And then I cast that flower away
To die and wither there;
But when I found it dead today
Why did I shed a tear?

O why are things so changed to me?
What gave me joy before
Now fills my heart with misery,
And nature smiles no more.

And why are all the beauties gone
From this my native hill?
Alas! my heart is changed alone:
Nature is constant still.

For when the heart is free from care,
Whatever meets the eye
Is bright, and every sound we hear
Is full of melody.

The sweetest strain, the wildest wind,
The murmur of a stream,
To the sad and weary mind
Like doleful death knells seem.

Father! thou hast long been dead,
Mother! thou art gone,
Brother! thou art far away,
And I am left alone.

Long before my mother died
I was sad and lone,
And when she departed too
Every joy was flown

But the world's before me now,
Why should I despair?
I will not spend my days in vain,
I will not linger here!

There is still a cherished hope
To cheer me on my way;
It is burning in my heart
With a feeble ray.

I will cheer the feeble spark
And raise it to a flame;
And it shall light me through the world,
And lead me on to fame.

I leave thee then, my childhood's home,
For all thy joys are gone;
I leave thee through the world to roam
In search of fair renown,

From such a hopeless home to part
Is happiness to me,
For nought can charm my weary heart
Except activity.

Poem 25

A Voice From the Dungeon

I'm buried now; I've done with life;
I've done with hate, revenge and strife;
I've done with joy, and hope and love
And all the bustling world above.

Long have I dwelt forgotten here
In pining woe and dull despair;
This place of solitude and gloom
Must be my dungeon and my tomb.

No hope, no pleasure can I find:
I am grown weary of my mind;
Often in balmy sleep I try
To gain a rest from misery,

And in one hour of calm repose
To find a respite from my woes,
But dreamless sleep is not for me
And I am still in misery.

I dream of liberty, 'tis true,
But then I dream of sorrow too,
Of blood and guilt and horrid woes,
Of tortured friends and happy foes;

I dream about the world, but then
I dream of fiends instead of men;
Each smiling hope so quickly fades
And such a lurid gloom pervades

That world - that when I wake and see
Those dreary phantoms fade and flee,
Even in my dungeon I can smile,
And taste of joy a little while.

And yet it is not always so;
I dreamt a little while ago
That all was as it used to be:
A fresh free wind passed over me;

It was a pleasant summer's day,
The sun shone forth with cheering ray,
Methought a little lovely child
Looked up into my face and smiled.

My heart was full, I wept for joy,
It was my own, my darling boy;
I clasped him to my breast and he
Kissed me and laughed in childish glee.

Just them I heard in whisper sweet
A well known voice my name repeat.
His father stood before my eyes;
I gazed at him in mute surprise,

I thought he smiled and spoke to me,
But still in silent ecstasy
I gazed at him; I could not speak;
I uttered one long piercing shriek.

Alas! Alas! That cursed scream
Aroused me from my heavenly dream;
I looked around in wild despair,
I called them, but they were not there;
The father and the child are gone,
And I must live and die alone.

Books For ALL Kinds of Readers

At ReadHowYouWant we understand that one size does not fit all types of readers. Our innovative, patent pending technology allows us to design new formats to make reading easier and more enjoyable for you. This helps improve your speed of reading and your comprehension. Our EasyRead printed books have been optimized to improve word recognition, ease eye tracking by adjusting word and line spacing as well as minimizing hyphenation. Our EasyRead SuperLarge editions have been developed to make reading easier and more accessible for vision-impaired readers. We offer Braille and DAISY formats of our books and all popular E-Book formats.

We are continually introducing new formats based upon research and reader preferences. Visit our web-site to see all of our formats and learn how you can Personalize our books for yourself or as gifts. Sign up to Become A RHYW Registered Reader.

www.readhowyouwant.com

Made in the USA
Lexington, KY
19 February 2012